SEN SUPERPOWERS

The Perfect Project
a book about autism

Written by
Dr. Tracy Packiam Alloway

Illustrated by
Ana Sanfelippo

Ms. James' class was preparing for the Science Fair.

"Today we're going to start making projects for the fair," she said. "There's a prize for first place!"

"Listen carefully—I'm going to call out the names in each group. You will need to choose a team leader and decide on a topic."

Charlie heard his name, but he was very busy. "Choo, choo," he said as he moved his train across his books. "Terrance the Train feels happy."

Emma, Matt, and Andrew were in Charlie's group. They made their way over to his desk.

"Let's build a train model for our project," suggested Emma.

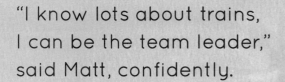
"I know lots about trains,
I can be the team leader,"
said Matt, confidently.

"I know a lot about trains, too.
I have a remote-control train
set at home," Andrew boasted.

"Real trains don't use remote
controls. They run on electricity
that they get from the track,"
Charlie said, reading his book.

The group started work on their train model.

"I think we can put this here," said Charlie. But as he reached over to attach the next piece, the model collapsed!

Liam burst out crying, "Oh no! The model
is ruined—now we won't win a prize."

"That's okay, we can start again."
Emma started picking up the pieces.

"We'll be able to build it faster
if we all lend a hand," Matt said.

But Charlie wasn't so sure...

"Charlie! Where are you going?"
said Andrew.

8

Charlie didn't answer.
He covered his ears
and ran away as fast
as he could.

Ms. James followed Charlie to the library.

"Is everything OK, Charlie?" she asked.

"Terrance the Train doesn't want to play anymore," said Charlie. "He doesn't want to lend his hand. He likes his hand and wants to keep it."

Ms. James understood why Charlie was upset and explained that 'lend a hand' also meant that each member of the team had to work together.

"Let's go back to the classroom together. Why don't you write down some facts for your group's presentation while the others finish the model?" said Ms. James, softly.

The next morning, Ms. James had some bad news. "I'm sorry, team, but Matt is sick and won't be able to make it to the fair tomorrow," she explained.

"Who will present our project now?" moaned Liam.

One of the fastest bullet trains in the world is in Japan and it goes up to 224 mph.

A Malaysian nicknamed 'King Tooth' won the record for pulling a train by his teeth.

The longest train ride in the world goes from Europe to Asia.

"Wow! Charlie, you know a lot about trains!" exclaimed Andrew. "Will you present our project?"

Charlie smiled and nodded.

When Ms. James's class arrived at the Science Fair, it was very busy and noisy.

Heels were clattering.
Chairs were squeaking.
Books were dropping.

"Where's Charlie?" asked Andrew.

Liam, Emma, and Andrew
looked everywhere.

"I think I see him!"
pointed Emma.

Charlie looked very worried.
He didn't like the noise.

"Here Charlie, try these," said Andrew,
giving Charlie some ear defenders.

Charlie put them on and smiled.
"Terrance the Train likes it when it is quiet."

Andrew understood that Charlie
felt calmer with his ear defenders on.

Soon it was time for Charlie's team to show their project to the judges. One by one, all the train facts came out of Charlie's mouth.

Facts about steam engines.
Facts about trains and electricity.
Facts about cargo trains and
passenger trains.

The more Charlie talked,
the more points the judges
gave them!

After the judges had seen all of the projects,
it was time for them to announce the winners.

Third place went to the rocket project...

...second, to the volcano project...

...and in first place...was Charlie's team with their train project!

"We won! We won!" whooped Liam.

"Charlie, you did it!" cheered Andrew.

Your amazing memory for train facts helped us win first place," said Emma.

NOTES FOR PARENTS AND TEACHERS

Autism is a developmental disability that can affect a variety of areas, including:

SOCIAL INTERACTION
Autism is characterized by a difficulty in recognizing and responding appropriately to social and emotional cues, which causes problems with social interactions.

EXPRESSING EMOTIONS
Children with autism can find it difficult to express their emotions. So, they may repeat phrases they have heard or use their favorite character to communicate what they feel, just as Charlie did when he talked about Terrance the Train.

SENSORY OVERLOAD
Students with autism may have good working memory but struggle to use it when they experience sensory overload, with loud noises, odd smells, or even certain lights. This can make it difficult for them to concentrate in crowded or noisy places.

MEMORY
Memory for facts and events is often very strong in children with autism. This powerful memory system can help them memorize not just interesting facts; but also rules to help them navigate social situations.

Autism is a complex condition with no two children the same, however it's important to consider the suitability of tasks that you give to an autistic child. They might find it tricky to express emotions, understand language, and deal with sensory overload, but, just like Charlie, children with autism have good working memory. This skill means that they are great at remembering facts and being knowledgeable about specific topics.

DISCUSSION POINTS ABOUT THE STORY

Explain to the children what autism is and that it can have an impact on social interactions, such as making friends and having conversations. Also talk about the positive aspects of having autism, such as having a great memory and being honest. Below are some discussion points about the story that will help children with their comprehension skills as well as developing their awareness of autism:

(pp 7-9) Charlie didn't understand that 'lend a hand' was just an expression. What do you do when you don't understand what someone means?

(pp 14-16) Charlie felt overwhelmed at the Science Fair. Have you been in a crowded place? How did it make you feel?

(p 17) When Charlie blocked out the noises with his ear defenders, he was able to calm down, then remember and talk about everything he knew about trains. Do you have special tricks to help you remember things?

(p 10) Charlie talks about Terrance the train to express his emotions. How do you express your feelings?

TIPS FOR COPING WITH AUTISM

Here are some handy tips to expand children's long-term memory and help them be superheroes like Charlie!

LIST IT
This game can increase how quickly children remember things because it keeps the link from their working memory to their long-term memory active. Ask them to list as many vegetables as they can in 10 seconds. Try it again, but this time listing fruits, colors, and so on.

LEARN BEFORE SNOOZING
Studies show that learning before bedtime can help our memory store the information safely and allow us to remember it better.

DRAW IT!
Studies show that 20 minutes of drawing can boost working memory. So encourage children to grab some coloring pencils and have fun!

CONNECT IT
Whether it's dinosaurs or robots, use a child's interests to promote learning by creating connections between new information and things they already know.

DRUM YOUR FINGERS
Tap or clap a rhythm and ask children to remember the sequence of taps.

Quarto is the authority on a wide range of topics. Quarto educates, entertains and enriches the lives of our readers—enthusiasts and lovers of hands-on living.
www.quartoknows.com

Author: Dr Tracy Packiam Alloway
Illustrator: Ana Sanfelippo
Editors: Emily Pither and Victoria Garrard
Designers: Victoria Kimonidou and Clare Barber
Consultant: Lorraine Peterson OBE

© 2019 Quarto Publishing plc

First published in 2019 by QEB Publishing, an imprint of The Quarto Group.
26391 Crown Valley Parkway, Suite 220
Mission Viejo, CA 92691.
T: +1 949 380 7510
F: +1 949 380 7575
www.QuartoKnows.com

A CIP record for this book is available from the Library of Congress.

ISBN 978-0-71124-328-6

9 8 7 6 5 4 3 2 1

Manufactured in Shenzhen, China PP082019

FSC
www.fsc.org
MIX
Paper from responsible sources
FSC® C001701

To Magnus, my train expert